E.B. CRAWFORD PUBLIC LIBRARY

3 2823 00115 0397

DISCARD

My daddy's amazing, just look and see.
There's so many amazing things he can be.

D1529957

He can be a pillow,
for me to rest my head

or he can do even better, and be a whole bed

He can be a crane
and lift me up very high

He can be a catapult, and toss me
up to the sky

He can be a car,
he can go vroom vroom

Ask your daddy to drive you
across the room

He can be a bull,
he can buck and he can snort

He can be a truck,
and help me build a great fort

Ask your daddy
if you can crawl on him

He can be a detective,
and find me when I hide

He can dance like a ballerina,
wearing a tutu

He can be a rocket launcher,
and throw me really far

Ask your daddy,
can he do the same thing?

When we're in a pool
he turns into a boat

And when I get tired,
he keeps me afloat

But of all the amazing
things he can be

My favorite thing of all is
when he's my daddy!

42801706R00020

Made in the USA
Middletown, DE
22 April 2017